Superfairies

Dancer the Wild Pony

by Janey Louise Jones

illustrated by Jennie Poh

PICTURE WINDOW BOOKS
a capstone imprint

Superfairies is published by Picture Window Books
A Capstone Imprint
1710 Roe Crest Drive
North Mankato, Minnesota 56003
www.mycapstone.com

Text © 2016 Janey Louise Jones
Illustrations © 2016 Jennie Poh

Library of Congress Cataloging-in-Publication Data

Jones, Janey, 1968- author
  Dancer the wild pony / by Janey Louise Jones ;
illustrated by Jennie Poh.
          pages cm. -- (Superfairies)
  Summary: The Summer Fair is coming up, and
Dancer the pony has run away because she does not
want to dance, and it is up to the Superfairies to give
her confidence--but first they have to catch her.
  ISBN 978-1-4795-8642-4 (library binding) -- ISBN
978-1-4795-8646-2 (pbk.) -- ISBN 978-1-4795-8650-
9 (ebook pdf)
1. Fairies--Juvenile fiction. 2. Ponies--Juvenile
fiction. 3. Anxiety--Juvenile fiction. 4. Self-
confidence--Juvenile fiction. 5. Dance--Juvenile
fiction. [1. Fairies--Fiction. 2. Ponies--Fiction. 3.
Anxiety--Fiction. 4. Self-confidence--Fiction. 5.
Dance--Fiction.] I. Poh, Jennie, illustrator. II. Title.
  PZ7.J72019Dan 2016
  [E]--dc23
                              2015031707

Designer: Alison Thiele

For my grandparents – Smudge and Dot x
– Jennie Poh

Printed and bound in US.
007522CGS16

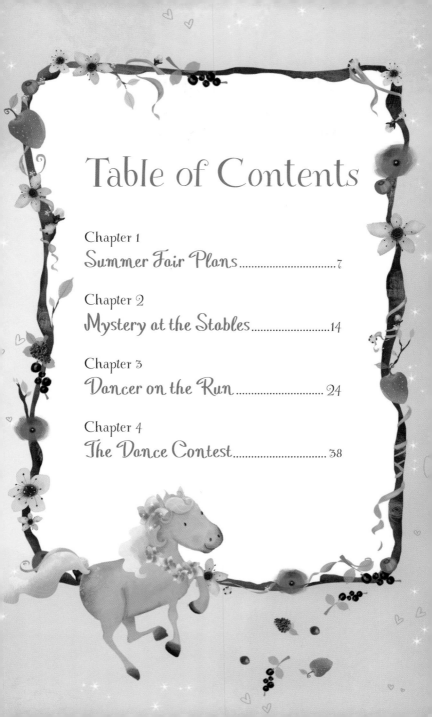

Table of Contents

The Fairy World

The Superfairies of Peaseblossom Woods use teamwork to rescue animals in trouble. They bring together their special superskills, petal power and lots of love.

Superfairy Rose
can blow super healing fairy kisses to make the animals in Peaseblossom Woods feel better.

Superfairy Berry

can see for miles
around with her
super eyesight.

Superfairy Star

can create super dazzling
brightness in one dainty spin
to lighten up dark places.

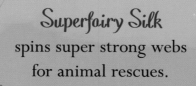

Superfairy Silk

spins super strong webs
for animal rescues.

Chapter 1

Summer Fair Plans

The sun was warm and bright, and the air was filled with the scent of roses and lavender. The river tinkled through Peaseblossom Woods, and the woodland animals relaxed in the soothing warmth of midsummer.

The Superfairies were very excited!

"Yippee! Today's the Summer Fair," said Rose. "It's always so much fun. I'm in charge of the contest to design the best fairy dress!"

"I can't wait. I'm going to sell superjams," said Berry. "I've been picking berries all week!"

"I'm going to help people make necklaces," said Star. She placed lots of sparkling gemstones in a box.

"The fair is always the best day of summer!" declared Rose. "I love seeing all the animals having fun."

"Let's decorate the cherry blossom tree with flowers and lanterns!" said Silk.

"Yes!" chorused the other three Superfairies.

"I *love* the dance contest at the fair!" said Star. "I so want to win this year!"

"Oh, Star. It's fun to take part, but you know Dancer the wild pony *always* wins," said Rose.

"Yes, she's a lovely dancer, the best in Peaseblossom Woods," said Star.

"But I won't give up hope," she added with a smile, as she practiced her dance moves around the house.

The fairies started to decorate their house with branches of delicate blossoms and vases of pink roses. Then they heard the sound of bells ringing in the woods.

Ting-aling-aling …

Ting-aling-aling …

They all stopped what they were doing immediately.

"Listen! One of the animals needs us!" cried Rose.

She checked the Strawberry computer.

"What's the problem?" asked Berry.

"We've got to get over to Copperwood Stables as fast as possible!" Rose said.

"Oh dear!" said Berry. "Can you see what's happening?"

"Yes!" cried Rose. "Dancer's in some kind of trouble. How terrible!"

"Dancer?" said Star. "Poor thing. I wonder what's going on. Let's get moving."

The fairies filled the tank of the fairycopter with spring water fuel from the pump, flew into their seats, checked their checklist, and were soon ready for take-off.

There was no time to waste when a rescue was required.

"5, 4, 3, 2, 1 ... go, go, go!" said Berry, at the controls.

The fairies were up in the air in the fairycopter in the swish of a flower wand.

"Perfect flying conditions," said Berry, at the controls. "Clear sky and no danger in sight. Hopefully this won't take long to figure out."

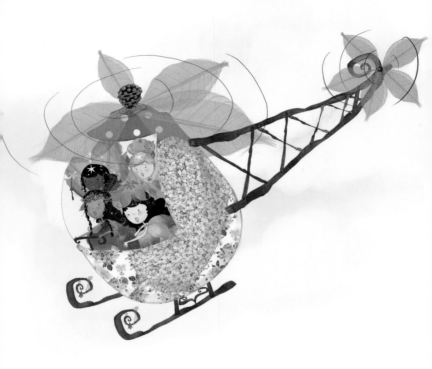

"I hope not," agreed Rose. "We need to get organized for the Summer Fair!"

The fairycopter fluttered over the leafy trees of Peaseblossom Woods.

Chapter 2

Mystery at the Stables

"There is Copperwood Stables down below," said Berry. She began to lower the fairycopter into a clearing in the woods. The fairies flew out of the fairycopter toward the stables.

Dancer's sister, Cloud, stood waiting for them at Copperwood Stables. She was alone.

"That's strange," said Rose. "Where's Dancer?"

The Superfairies all looked across the field for Dancer, but there was no sign of her.

"I'm so happy to see you," called
Cloud, as the fairycopter landed. "The
thing is—Dancer has disappeared!"

"Disappeared? That's odd! Maybe she's
just on an errand? When did you last see
her?" asked Star.

"She was dancing away in the field,
then I heard her sobbing. Loud, sad sobs.
I came to find out what was wrong," said
Cloud.

"Go on," urged Silk.

"I saw her cantering off toward the woods, throwing up dust behind her as she went," explained Cloud.

"How strange. She loves the dance contest at the Summer Fair," said Star. "I wonder why she was so upset."

"I don't understand what happened," said Cloud. "It's not like her at all."

"Can you think of anywhere she might have gone?" asked Rose.

"Well, she often has her hair decorated with flowers by the squirrels at their beauty parlor, so you could try there," suggested Cloud.

"Okay. Let's start at Squirrel Square," said Rose.

The fairies flew westward to where the squirrel family lived.

The squirrels were busy packing
things for the Beauty Stall at the Summer
Fair. They piled in strawberry shampoo,
petal perfume, blueberry cream, and
sandalwood soap. These were just some
of the lovely things the squirrels made for
everyone in Peaseblossom Woods.

Mrs. Squirrel came out to greet the Superfairies.

"Hello! I thought I heard the bells ring. How can I help you?" asked Mrs. Squirrel.

"Have you seen Dancer?" asked Silk.

"Not recently. We often put flowers in her mane, especially before dance contests. But not today, funnily enough," said Mrs. Squirrel. "Try the Frogs' house. She often chats with Mr. Frog."

"Will do, thanks Mrs. Squirrel!" said Silk.

The fairies flew immediately over to the riverbank and explained what had happened.

"Dancer's gone missing?" said Mr. Frog, with a look of shock. "That's very surprising!"

"She often likes to look at her reflection in the pond and chat with me about this and that," Mr. Frog continued, "but not today. Why not try the Mousey House? The mice said they had been talking to her about the dance contest."

At the Mousey House, Little Miss Mouse was busy fixing a bow in her hair.

"Oh, hi Superfairies!" she cried.

But she was soon very upset to hear about Dancer.

"Gone missing? Oh no!" said Little Miss Mouse. "She was here yesterday. She said her dance wasn't good enough to win this year. I told her to practice and just do her best. I watched her dance, and told her she did a lovely job, but she didn't sound as if she believed me."

The Superfairies began to get worried.

"Oh, how worrying," said Rose. "Can you think of *anywhere* else she may have gone to?"

"Hmmm, possibly to Badger's Dell. She likes to go there sometimes to see what Belinda Badger thinks of her dances," said Little Miss Mouse.

Over at Badger's Dell, the Superfairies saw dainty hoof-prints in the ground.

"A clue at last!" said Silk.

"Let's follow the hoof-prints!" said Berry.

The hoof-prints were almost certainly Dancer's. They looked as if Dancer had been upset. The prints went this way, then that way, then round in circles.

Finally, the hoof-prints stopped at the door of the Badger House.

Berry knocked on the door.

Chapter 3

Dancer on the Run

"Hello! Anybody home?" she called, peering in the window.

Mrs. Badger opened the door. "Yes?" she said, rather sharply.

"Hello, have you seen Dancer?" asked Silk.

"Um, no, I haven't. Sorry, can't help you," said Mrs. Badger, slamming the door shut.

The Superfairies were suspicious. Mrs. Badger was usually so friendly.

There was a whinnying sound from inside the house.

"Her hoof-prints stop here. I can hear her. She *has* to be in there," said Berry.

"But why is she hiding—and how do we get her out?" wondered Rose.

"I'll try to see what's going on inside the house," said Star. She peered in the little window. "I can't see a thing," she complained.

"Let me try," said Berry, squeezing in next to Star. "I *do* see Dancer! And Belinda too."

"What are they doing?" asked Rose curiously.

"Dancer looks very sad. Her head is low and her eyes are glistening. She's been crying, I'd say," said Berry.

"If they won't let us in, we will have to get them out somehow," said Rose.

"Why don't I dazzle, and they'll all come outside to see what's going on," said Star.

"Good idea. It's worth a try," said Rose.

Star spun around, creating a big bright flash.

Twinkle. Sparkle. Dazzle. Tada!

The bright light dazzled in the dell. All the badgers came racing outside to see what was going on.

"We know she's in there," said Star. "Why won't she come out?"

"We can't tell you," said Mrs. Badger.

"You must! Cloud is worried and so are we," said Silk.

Mrs. Badger clearly wanted to help. She dropped her voice to a whisper. "She's worried about the dance contest—says she's forgotten how to dance. Got herself worked up, poor dear. Doesn't want to be in it this year, she says."

At that very moment, Dancer clip-clopped out of the house, heading toward the woods. She gathered speed and in a blink was racing into the distance. Powdery dust filled the air behind her.

"Dancer, come back!" called Silk. "Please! We can help you!"

But Dancer galloped wildly through the woods, while the Superfairies chased after her from the air above.

"Look out, Dancer!" cried Berry. "There's a huge hedge up ahead!"

Dancer cantered faster and faster. She jumped over the hedge ... then landed safely on the other side ... and carried on running.

She ran ... and ran ... and ran ...

She came to Rabbit Ridge.

The rabbits were icing their huge carrot cake for the home-baking stall at the Summer Fair.

"Ah, that looks lovely!" said Mrs. Rabbit, wiping her brow as she stood back to admire her work. "I think that might be my best ever!"

Dancer galloped along so fast that she couldn't slow down.

"Dancer! Be careful!" cried Star. "You have to stop!"

Dancer was racing toward Mrs. Rabbit's carrot cake.

Her eyes were misty with tears and she couldn't see well.

Mrs. Rabbit heard Dancer and turned around in time to see the sad little pony careering toward her—and her cake!

"Watch my cake!" cried Mrs. Rabbit.

Too late!

Dancer ran over the cake.

Squelch. Splodge. Splatter.

Dancer kept running.

Mrs. Rabbit looked up at the Superfairies. "You've got to stop her before she does any more damage!" she called. "I spent hours on this cake!"

The Superfairies could see that Dancer was going to run until she couldn't run any more.

Dancer kept cantering. The Superfairies kept flying. Everyone was exhausted. But how could they get Dancer to stop?

Dancer came to a clearing that had five paths leading from it.

She seemed to hesitate for a moment.

"Perhaps she will stop here," said Rose.

Dancer decided to take the narrowest, trickiest path into the deepest part of the woods.

The Superfairies needed all their skills to follow her down the dark path and dodge between the branches.

Eventually, Dancer stumbled.

"What shall we do?" asked Star. "Her poor little legs!"

"Silk, you'll have to catch her gently in a web," called Rose. "We can't talk to her while she's out of control like this."

As Dancer stumbled along a narrow path between the tress, Silk dropped a web in front of her.

Dancer couldn't go to the left ... and she couldn't go to the right.

She came to a stop as the web folded around her.

"Leave me alone!" she cried. "I don't want help! I don't want to go to the stupid Summer Fair!"

"We want to help because we care about you!" said Rose, blowing a healing kiss.

"I'm no good at dancing now!" Dancer cried. "Please don't make me dance!"

Rose's kiss landed on Dancer's pretty nose. She settled down after that.

"Come on, Dancer. You're the greatest dancer in Peaseblossom Woods. We *need* you at the Summer Fair!" said Star.

"I can't do it!" sobbed Dancer. "It's horrible when everyone *expects* you to be the best every year. I am so nervous!"

"Oh, you poor thing," said Rose. "Why don't you dance with Star this year?"

Dancer's face broke into a sweet little smile.

"I suppose I could try that," agreed Dancer. "It would be lovely to dance with her—if she wants to."

"I'd love to!" said Star. "It would be an honor."

Dancer giggled. "This could be fun!" she said.

Rose was relieved—she had been so worried that Dancer would get hurt. But she was safe and well. And with any luck, she would still be in the dance contest.

Chapter 4

The Dance Contest

Before the Summer Fair, Star and Dancer had a picnic lunch by the cherry blossom tree.

"What should we do for our dance?" asked Star.

"I've been practicing something special," said Dancer. "Do you want to see?"

"Yes, let's go further along the riverbank and try out some moves," suggested Star.

"That's great," said Dancer. "After that, would you like to come with me to have flowers put in our hair?"

"Oooh, I'd love that," said Star.

Dancer and Star had their hair done with matching pink flowers.

Everyone in Peaseblossom Woods was happy and calm as the Summer Fair began. All of the animals arrived with baskets and food and decorations and balloons. The young animals enjoyed playing games. The moms and dads chatted and ate cupcakes. Mr. Otter took barge trips along the river.

At last, it was time for the dance contest.

A huge audience gathered to see Star and Dancer dance together.

They danced a scene from *Cinderella*.

Mr. Badger played on an old piano.

Dancer and Star made dainty jumps, spins and hops.

It was the prettiest dance anyone had ever seen.

"Well done!" said Rose. "That was truly lovely."

Dancer was so nervous when it was time for the winner to be announced that all the fairies hovered around her to make sure she didn't run off again.

"And the winner is …" announced Mr Mouse. "Ah, we have two winners this year—Star and Dancer!"

A huge cheer went up in the crowd.

"Best dance ever," said someone.

"A lovely partnership!" said another.

"How sweet," said Little Miss Mouse.

"Hey, we both won this year!" laughed Star, as they received floral garlands from Mr. Mouse.

The four Superfairies lay back on the grass with the sun shining on them.

Dancer turned to all the Superfairies. "Thank you for giving me back my confidence," she said. "I'm sorry I've tired everyone out!

"Phew, we are tired," said Rose. "But it's time for our song!"

The Superfairies formed a fairy circle, while Dancer danced in the middle. The fairies sang their rescue song.

Dancer danced merrily along the riverbank.

"Hey, come back!" called Rose.

Dancer cantered straight back. And she promised not to run away the next time she felt nervous!

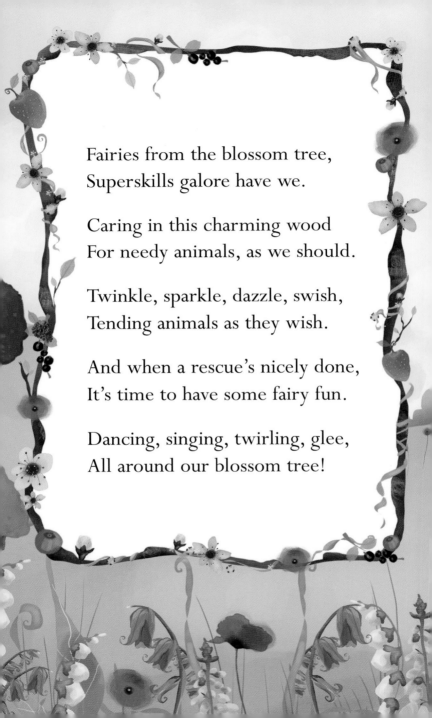

Fairies from the blossom tree,
Superskills galore have we.

Caring in this charming wood
For needy animals, as we should.

Twinkle, sparkle, dazzle, swish,
Tending animals as they wish.

And when a rescue's nicely done,
It's time to have some fairy fun.

Dancing, singing, twirling, glee,
All around our blossom tree!

Glossary

canter (KAN-tur)—a smooth run by a horse

confidence (KON-fuh-denss)—belief in yourself

dell (DELL)—small valley among trees

garland (GAR-luhnd)—wreath of flowers or leaves

honor (ON-ur)—great respect

lantern (LAN-turn)—movable light

nervous (NUR-vuhss)—easily agitated or alarmed

scent (SENT)—perfume or odor

sooth (SOOTH) — gently calm

Talk It Out

1. If you were at the Summer Fair in Peaseblossom Woods, which activities would you like to do? Can you think of another activity they could have at the Summer Fair?

2. Dancer doesn't want to be found, but why do the Superfairies want to rescue her anyway? Do you think Dancer was right to run away? Why?

3. How do you think Mrs. Rabbit felt after her beautiful cake was destroyed? Why is it important to respect the work people put into things?

Write It Down

1. Make a poster for the Summer Fair. Use details from the book for your description of the fair.

2. Write a short letter from Cloud, begging Dancer to come home.

3. Explain why Dancer got so nervous.

All About Fairies

The legend of fairies is as old as time. Fairy tales tell stories of fairy magic. According to legend, fairies are so small and delicate, and fly so fast, that they might actually be all around us, but just very hard to see. Fairies, supposedly, only reveal themselves to believers.

Fairies often dance in circles at sunrise and sunset. They love to play in woodlands among wildflowers. If you sing gently to them, they may very well appear.

Here are some of the world's most famous fairies:

The Flower Fairies

Artist Cicely Mary Barker painted a range of pretty flower fairies and published eight volumes of flower fairy art from 1923. The link between fairies and flowers is very strong.

The Tooth Fairy

She visits us during the night to leave a coin when we lose our baby teeth. Although it is very hard to catch sight of her, children are always happy when she visits.

Fake Fairies

In 1917, cousins Elsie Wright and Frances Griffiths said they photographed fairies in their garden. They later admitted that most were fakes—but Frances claimed that one was genuine.

Which Superfairy Are You?

1. What is your favorite color?
   A) purple
   B) pink
   C) red
   D) yellow

2. What is your favorite shape?
   A) diamond
   B) circle
   C) triangle
   D) star

3. If someone was upset, would you …
   A) give them help
   B) blow kisses
   C) make a small gift
   D) make them smile

4. For fun, do you like to …
   A) play games
   B) dress up
   C) bake cakes with a grown-up
   D) dance

5. Which food sounds tastiest to you?
   A) lavender cupcakes
   B) rose petal biscuits
   C) strawberry ice cream
   D) golden sponge cake

6. Which type of jewelry do you like best?
   A) rings
   B) heart-shaped lockets
   C) bracelets
   D) beads

7. What kind of book do you prefer to read?
   A) adventure
   B) fairytale
   C) nonfiction
   D) funny

8. What is your favorite flower?
   A) lily
   B) rose
   C) daisy
   D) daffodil

Mostly A—you are like Silk. Adventurous and brave, you always think of ways to deal with problems! You enjoy action and adventures.

Mostly B—you are like Rose: gentle, kind and loving. You are good at staying calm and love pink things.

Mostly C—you are like Berry: good fun, always helpful, with lots of great ideas. You are sensible and wise.

Mostly D—you are like Star. You cheer people up and dazzle with your sparkling ways! You are funny and enjoy jokes and dancing.

About the Author

Janey Louise Jones has been a published author for 10 years. Her Princess Poppy series is an international bestselling brand, with books translated into 10 languages, including Hebrew and Mandarin. Janey is a graduate of Edinburgh University and lives in Edinburgh, Scotland with her three sons. She loves fairies, princesses, beaches, and woodlands.

About the Illustrator

Jennie Poh was born in England and grew up in Malaysia (in the jungle). At the age of 10 she moved back to England and trained as a ballet dancer. She studied fine art at Surrey Institute of Art & Design as well as fashion illustration at Central Saint Martins. Jennie loves the countryside, animals, tea, and reading. She lives in Woking, England with her husband and two wonderful daughters.